Puffin Books

# MARZIPAN MAX

When Herr Gross, the elderly baker, teaches Max how to make marzipan, little does he realize what he has started. Max's beautiful marzipan animals and fruit are real works of art and everyone in his little mountain village in Switzerland loves them. Max's marzipan models are such a success that they decide to enter a national competition. They set off for St Moritz with Max's wonderful creations, but all does not quite go as planned. So how does Max achieve fame and fortune for his village?

Alexander McCall Smith was born in Zimbabwe and obtained a Bachelor of Law degree from the University of Rhodesia. He then went to Scotland and received his doctorate in philosophy at Edinburgh University. He now lectures in law at Edinburgh and has written numerous books for children.

# MARZIPAN MAX

## Alexander McCall Smith

### Illustrated by Toni Goffe

PUFFIN BOOKS

This book is for Naomi, Misa,
Michiko and Kiyoshi Yamanaka

PUFFIN BOOKS

Published by the Penguin Group
Penguin Books Ltd, 27 Wrights Lane, London W8 5TZ, England
Penguin Books USA Inc., 375 Hudson Street, New York, New York 10014, USA
Penguin Books Australia Ltd, Ringwood, Victoria, Australia
Penguin Books Canada Ltd, 10 Alcorn Avenue, Toronto, Ontario, Canada M4V 3B2
Penguin Books (NZ) Ltd, 182–190 Wairau Road, Auckland 10, New Zealand

Penguin Books Ltd, Registered Offices: Harmondsworth, Middlesex, England

First published by Blackie & Son Ltd 1991
Published in Puffin Books 1993
1 3 5 7 9 10 8 6 4 2

Text copyright © Alexander McCall Smith, 1991
Illustrations copyright © Toni Goffe, 1991

The moral right of the author has been asserted

Printed in England by Clays Ltd, St Ives plc

# 1 The Old Baker

*Marzipan!* I shall always remember the smell of it as I walked into that village, high in the mountains of Switzerland. There was nothing else it could have been – somebody was making marzipan!

It was not a large village. There was a tiny grocery shop, with milk churns stacked outside it, a post office, and a square church with a white clock tower. And then, as I turned the corner, the enticing smell of marzipan became stronger until suddenly, right before me,

5

was the marzipan shop.

Later, I asked the people in the village how it was that such a small place, so far from anywhere, should have a shop that sold only marzipan.

'It's a very strange story,' they said. 'Would you like to hear it?'

I nodded. 'Of course I would.'

So they told me the remarkable tale of Max, Herr Gross, and the wonderful, wonderful marzipan. And here it is.

Max lived with his father and mother at the very edge of the village. His father was a farmer and their house, like all the other houses in that area, was really half-barn and half-house. In the cold winters, when the mountain-sides and the valley floor were covered with a thick layer of snow, the cows and the sheep took shelter in the barn side of the house. As he lay in

bed at night, Max could hear the sound of the animals in their stalls. It was a comforting sound that always made him feel drowsy and safe.

When the snow melted in the late spring, the animals would be taken up on to the high mountain pastures. There they would stay for months on end, until the cold winds came again and the first sign of snow could be seen in the sky.

Just about everyone in the village was a farmer, too. Everyone, that is, except for the postman, the grocer, and Herr Gross. Herr Gross was a baker, and the village people were very proud of him. Not every village had its own baker, and people would come from all the neighbouring villages up and down the valley to buy the bread baked by Herr Gross.

Max loved to watch Herr Gross mixing the dough for the bread. Sometimes he would help dust each loaf with flour before the large trays were slid into the wood-fired oven. Then, when the bread was done, they would tip it on to racks and leave it to cool until the customers came for it.

'You should become a baker,' Herr Gross said to him. 'You could make a good living.'

'Would you teach me?' Max asked.

Herr Gross laughed. 'I'm too old,' he replied. 'It's as much as I can do to keep up with the demand for my bread. And I can't go on forever!'

Max loved the taste of Herr Gross's bread, and he wondered if the old man was able to make anything else. If he made such delicious bread, then surely he should be able to bake cakes and biscuits. So he asked Herr Gross one day if he ever made Christmas cakes.

Herr Gross frowned. 'I haven't made a cake for years,' he said. 'I suppose I could still do it.'

'What about biscuits?' Max asked. 'Could you make those, too?'

'If I had to,' said Herr Gross. Then he paused before going on. 'I'll tell you what I was really good at – marzipan. I used to make it when I was learning my trade. My boss was a marvellous marzipan maker – the best in the country, I think. And he taught me some of his tricks. I've never forgotten them, although that was an awful long time ago.'

Max caught his breath.

'Marzipan?' There was nothing he loved to eat more than marzipan. Rich, yellow marzipan, smelling of almonds and tasting even more delicious than chocolate itself. The very thought of it made Max's mouth water.

Herr Gross looked at Max. There was a smile on his face as he dusted his hands on his apron.

'Would you like some?' he asked suddenly.

'There's nothing I'd like more,' Max answered quickly. 'Nothing!'

It took Herr Gross some time to find the ingredients, but at last he had them all

assembled. He poured out a pile of
almonds and deftly crushed them into a
paste. Then he added vanilla, and sugar,
and one or two other things besides.
Finally, humming as he worked, he
pounded the paste into a thin sheet and
smoothed it into the bottom of a
saucepan.

A few minutes later, Herr Gross took the saucepan off his cooker and peered at the contents.

'Just perfect,' he announced.

And it was. The moment the thick, half-crumbly paste touched his tongue, Max realized that this was the tastiest marzipan he had ever come across.

Herr Gross beamed with pleasure as he saw Max's expression.

'Here,' he said, rolling the rest of the marzipan into a thickish block. 'Take it home and make some marzipan pigs out of it!'

## 2   A Trip is Planned

Max carefully wrapped up the large block of marzipan and took it home. He was tempted to eat more of it on the way – terribly tempted – but Herr Gross's words came back to him and he did not break off so much as a crumb of it. Max had seen marzipan animals in shop windows before, and the idea of making some himself was an appealing one.

That evening, Max made a cow and a pig. He modelled them carefully, using tiny drops of colouring liquid from the kitchen at home to make the marzipan different shades. The cow was brown, with black patches and horns. The pig was pink all over, but wore a white collar and had a scarlet nose. Max was very proud of both of them.

The next day Max used up the rest of the marzipan making a whole flock of sheep, a long line of marzipan ducks, and a family of stout pigs. He was pleased

with the results and that afternoon he placed all the animals carefully on a tray and took them off to show Herr Gross.

'Remarkable!' exclaimed Herr Gross as Max showed him his handiwork. 'Yes, quite remarkable!'

Herr Gross picked up the marzipan cow gently and examined it from all angles.

'This is wonderful,' he said, after he had placed it back alongside the other pieces. 'Max, we must make some more. People are going to love these!'

Max's mouth fell open. 'You mean that people might actually buy them?'

Herr Gross nodded. 'Of course they'll buy them. You could take them round the village and sell every one of them. Just you try!'

Max felt a little bit shy about carrying his stock of marzipan animals to people's houses, but he soon found that everybody was delighted to see them. At the first house at which he called, they bought the cow and one of the ducks.

'It's my daughter's birthday tomorrow,' said the woman who bought them. 'They will be ideal presents for her.'

Max slipped the money into his pocket and made his way towards the next house. They bought a sheep and a pig, as did the people in the house after that. And so it continued until every last marzipan animal had been sold.

Back at the bakery, Max told Herr Gross that he had been right. Everybody had loved the marzipan.

'Here's the money,' he said, fishing a heavy handful of coins out of his pocket and handing it to the baker.

Herr Gross looked at the coins and shook his head. 'It's yours,' he said. 'You made them. You can keep all the money as long as. . .' He looked about the bakery. 'As long as you help me tidy this place up. It could do with a good sort out.'

When they had finished cleaning the bakery, Herr Gross sat down on the chair he kept near the oven door and looked thoughtfully at Max.

'That marzipan,' he began. 'Would you like to make some more?'

Max was delighted by the suggestion.

'You see,' went on Herr Gross, 'we could make a batch of marzipan on Saturdays and put it in the window for sale. I'm sure that we could sell ten or twelve pieces every week – as long as you don't mind making it into models.'

'I'd love to do that,' Max said. 'I could try all sorts of shapes. What about marzi-

pan fruit? I've seen red marzipan strawberries before.'

Herr Gross held up a hand to stop him.
'Not so fast,' he said. 'We'll have to get
the right ingredients, you know. We're
not going to sell any old marzipan – it's
got to be the very best.'

As Max listened, Herr Gross explained
that the secret of really fine marzipan was
to get the right almonds.

'And we should have to buy those from

over there,' he said, tossing his head in the direction of the mountains behind the village. Just on the other side of the mountain ridge lay the border, and beyond that was Italy.

'Nobody grows better almonds than the Italians,' Herr Gross explained. 'It might be the weather, or the soil, or even the way the Italians pick them; but they're always the best.'

'We could easily go there,' Max said eagerly. 'It's only an hour or two away.'

Herr Gross looked doubtful. 'You know what my old car's like,' he said. 'I don't know if Putti can still cope with these mountain roads.'

Max smiled. Everybody in the village knew Putti, Herr Gross's old car. He used it only once a week, to go down into the town at the end of the valley, and everybody heard the banging and clattering as it struggled to make the journey.

'Come on, Herr Gross,' Max urged. 'If we took it slowly, Putti could do it.'

Herr Gross scratched his head doubtfully.

'The roads are still quite icy,' he said. 'Perhaps we should wait until the spring.'

Max thought of the marzipan plan. The idea of modelling so much marzipan was such an exciting one that he could not bear the thought of waiting.

'Please, Herr Gross,' he said. 'If Putti stops, I'll get out and push. I promise!'

Herr Gross laughed. 'You may have to,' he said. 'My old legs aren't up to it.'

'Then we can go?' asked Max gleefully.

'If you really want to,' said Herr Gross. 'Yes, we can go.'

'When?' demanded Max.

Herr Gross shrugged. 'Next Saturday?'

# 3   On the Mountain-side

Next Saturday seemed very slow in coming, but at last Max found himself in the passenger seat of Herr Gross's old car while the baker tried to start the engine. It took several attempts, but at last Putti's engine coughed into life and they were off.

It was an extremely uncomfortable ride. It may be that Putti had springs once, but she certainly had none now. Every bump in the road, every little unexpected hump, made the old car rattle

and creak. And inside, the wind whistled through all sorts of holes and cracks.

'It's just as well I wrapped up warmly,' thought Max, as an icy gust eddied up around his ankles.

Slowly they made their way along the road that climbed up out of the valley along the mountainside. The road twisted like a bent pin, snaking its way through the steep, snowy forests. Putti's engine strained and groaned with the effort, but at last they came to the top of the pass and Max was able to look back at the village far below them.

Here the road forked. One way led off to St Moritz, the famous ski-town, with its expensive shops and grand hotels; the other led down into Italy. They stopped for a while at the junction, allowing the engine to cool after its effort. Then, with a cheerful whistle on his lips, Herr Gross

started the car again and they began to roll their way down into Italy.

Less than an hour later they were in the Italian market town where Herr Gross knew that almonds could be bought. Max had never been over the border before, and he found it all very different from Switzerland.

They tried two shops without success. One of them sold almonds, but Herr Gross examined them and shook his head.

'Not good enough,' he said to Max. 'We'll try elsewhere.'

So they made their way into more shops until at last the baker found exactly what he was after. The shopkeeper measured out a quantity of almonds and tipped them into a large bag. Then, the almond bag slung over Max's shoulder, the two walked back through the narrow streets to Putti.

'We've just got time for a cup of hot chocolate,' said Herr Gross, glancing at his watch. He pointed to a little café nearby and soon he and Max were enjoying a cup of steaming, milky hot chocolate – hot enough to keep them warm all the way back to Switzerland.

Putti found it very hard going chugging up the steep road on the Italian side of the mountain. The way here was more dangerous, as there were occasional places where the ice had frozen into large patches on the road. The valiant old car, though, seemed determined to take the journey in its stride, and although the engine coughed and spluttered from time to time it did not stop.

They were half-way up the mountain-side when Max heard the noise. It was a roaring sound, rather like a waterfall, or a mountain stream in full spate. To somebody who lived in the mountains, though, it meant only one thing – an avalanche!

An avalanche can happen on a mountain without any warning. When there is enough snow, and it is lying heavy enough, the slightest movement can set it off. Somewhere, high on the mountain-side above them, a wild animal had scurried through a snow bank, or a rock had

fallen, or a drift of snow had toppled, with the result that a great, crashing wave of snow and ice had begun to hurtle down to the roadway below.

'Herr Gross!' Max shouted as he saw the avalanche gathering speed. 'Look!'

When he saw the danger they were in, Herr Gross gasped and slammed his foot down on the accelerator. Putti's engine raced as the car shot forward, desperately trying to gather speed. If they only managed to get high enough, Herr Gross thought, they would be out of the avalanche's path, and safe.

Suddenly, it was too much for Putti. With a sigh, the engine stopped – just like that – and the car ground to a halt. Herr Gross struggled to start it again, frantically pressing the starter button, but it was to no avail. The very heart of the old car had failed.

'We must get out,' Herr Gross cried out. 'Quick! If we run up the road we might get out of the way in time.'

Max opened his door and leapt out. As he did so, he snatched the bag of almonds that had been lying at his feet.

'Don't bother with that!' Herr Gross cried. 'There's no time!'

But Max had already shouldered the bag and started off behind Herr Gross. In spite of his age, the old baker ran quickly,

and it was as much as Max could do to keep up with him.

'Hurry!' urged Herr Gross, casting a glance behind him. 'I don't think we're going to make it.'

Max looked up at the mountain. The sound of the approaching avalanche was now deafening, and he could see clouds of white powdery snow shooting up into the sky above the tree tops.

Now the sound was an almighty roar,

and Max was convinced that at any moment they would be crushed. Herr Gross gestured to him quickly, and they both threw themselves down on the roadside, sheltering their heads with their hands.

The ground shook beneath them as boulders, snow and tree trunks hurtled downwards. But suddenly the noise seemed below them and they realised that they were safe. Max sat up and looked down the road, just in time to see the avalanche cascade into Herr Gross's old car and sweep it away. Down the mountainside the old car slid and tumbled, now sideways, now upside down, like an abandoned and overturned toboggan.

Herr Gross watched sadly as his old friend Putti disappeared. Max turned towards him and saw a tear appear in his friend's eye.

'I had that car for over thirty years,' Herr Gross said sadly. 'I'll never get one like that again.'

# 4   More Marzipan is Made

They were picked up only a few minutes later by a lorry which had narrowly missed the avalanche. The lorry driver was able to drop them off in the village, and the news soon spread of Max and Herr Gross's narrow escape.

Everybody was very sorry to hear of the loss of Putti.

'That old car was quite a character,' Max's father said. 'But I'm very relieved that you weren't still in it when the avalanche arrived!'

Max admitted that he had been terribly frightened at the time, but he soon forgot all about it and began to think of what to do when the next batch of marzipan was made. This time, Herr Gross showed him how to make the marzipan himself, and slowly, by trial and error, Max began to produce marzipan which was almost as good as Herr Gross's. At last the baker tasted a batch and clapped his hands together.

'That's it, Max!' he said. 'You can now make marzipan just as I taught you to make it.'

Max was delighted, and now that he had got the recipe sorted out he began work on a trayful of marzipan pieces. Most of them were animals – marzipan pigs and ducks (which he made particularly well), but there were also pieces of marzipan fruit. There were delicious marzipan bananas, much smaller than the real ones, of course, but twice as tasty! There were marzipan strawberries, flavoured with strawberry essence and extraordinarily delicious. And, finally, there were marzipan apples, red and shiny, with a tiny green marzipan stalk at the top. Everything was beautifully made.

That Saturday, Herr Gross put the tray of Max's marzipan out in his window. He had expected it to last at least a week, but

within two hours every last piece of marzipan had been sold.

'It's indescribably delicious,' said the postman's wife, as she sank her teeth into a marzipan apple. 'I hope that Max makes more.'

'Of course he will,' Herr Gross reassured her. 'In fact, if you order some now I'm sure that he will have them ready for you by Monday.'

The postman's wife swallowed the last morsel of her marzipan apples.

'I think I'll have ten marzipan apples,' she said. 'Just like the one I've just eaten.'

Herr Gross began to write the order down, but was interrupted by the postman's wife.

'On second thoughts,' she said, a rather greedy glint appearing in her eye. 'Make that twenty!'

★ ★ ★

The marzipan proved so popular in the village that Max soon found most of his spare time being taken up by modelling the pieces. He didn't mind this, though, as working with marzipan seemed a delicious thing to do, even if you did not actually eat very much of it yourself.

Some weeks later, as Max was taking a pan of marzipan off the cooker, the baker passed him a magazine that he was read-

ing. It was a special magazine, read only by bakers and confectioners, full of news about flour and icing, and things like that.

'Read this,' said Herr Gross, pointing to a small article on an inner page. 'It's given me an idea.'

Max began to read. The article was all about the annual competition of the Guild of Swiss Confectioners. This year it was to be held in St Moritz, which was quite close by, and entry forms had to be submitted the following week.

'Why don't we enter some of your marzipan?' Herr Gross asked. 'I'm sure that it's good enough to win.'

Max was excited by the idea, but at the same time he felt a little bit nervous. The thought of competing against the finest Swiss sweet and chocolate makers was not something to be taken lightly. Herr Gross, though, became increasingly determined the more he thought about it.

'Yes,' he said firmly. 'It's about time this village got on the map. We'll enter – and we'll win!'

The competition was due to be held two weeks later, and during this time Max spent a great deal of time planning his entries. He was allowed to enter four pieces, and he decided that there would be two animals and two pieces of fruit. As far as the ingredients were concerned, Herr Gross had written off for a fresh supply of Italian almonds and some special essences from Germany. These arrived with a few days in hand, and so the day before the competition everything was ready for the important business of making and modelling the marzipan.

Herr Gross cancelled all baking for that day.

'I'm sorry,' he told his customers. 'Nothing's being baked today. There's something much, much more important about to happen!'

# 5 Bitter Disappointment

Taking great care to get the quantities just right, Herr Gross and Max mixed the marzipan ingredients in his best mixing-bowl. Then, when the paste was exactly right, they carefully rolled it out and put it in a pan. For the next few minutes, both Herr Gross and Max looked anxiously at their watches so that the marzipan should soften on the heat for just as long as was necessary, and no more.

At last it was ready, and Herr Gross

took the saucepan off with a flourish.

'The smell's perfect,' he said, sniffing the delicious odour that wafted from the newly-prepared delicacy.

Max waited impatiently until the mixture was cool, and then, trembling with excitement, he prised it out of the saucepan and began the task of modelling.

He had decided to make a marzipan pig (which was traditional) and then, to

add a touch of novelty, he had planned a marzipan whale. The pig went well. He dyed some marzipan the right shade of pink and then he slipped a tiny gold ring (made of marzipan, of course) through the pig's nose. Then he turned to the whale.

The top part of the whale was coloured black, the bottom part white. The whale's mouth was open, and inside was red

marzipan and tiny white marzipan teeth.
And from the whale's blow-hole on the
top of its head there spewed forth a white
marzipan fountain of foam.

Herr Gross inspected the animals the
moment Max announced that he was finished. For a moment he said nothing, and
Max wondered whether his marzipan had
lived up to his friend's expectations.
Then Herr Gross spoke.

'Marvellous!' he said. 'In fact, I've

never seen such marvellous marzipan animals in my life. We're going to win! I know it!'

Encouraged by this praise, Max then made two pieces of marzipan fruit – a marzipan orange and a bunch of marzipan grapes. These too were closely inspected by Herr Gross and passed as perfect.

They travelled into St Moritz by bus, the four marzipan pieces carefully stored in a box, which Max kept on his lap. As they came into the bustling town, Max felt overwhelmed by the wealth and glamour of it all. The people in the street were all dressed fashionably, with fur coats and expensive-looking gloves. Surely he and Herr Gross – two simple people from a little village in the mountains – would stand no chance in a competition in a place like this.

It was as if Herr Gross had read Max's

thoughts. As they went into the exhibition hall where the competition was to be held, the old baker turned to Max and whispered in his ear.

'Don't worry,' he said. 'These people may look very grand, but they're just the same as you or I underneath it all!'

Most of the entries in the competition were from chocolate makers. In the mar-

zipan section, though, there were four entries apart from theirs – two from confectioners in St Moritz, one from Zürich, and one from a confectioner who had come all the way from Geneva.

Herr Gross handed over their box and watched the officials lay out the four pieces on a table.

'Very nice,' the official said, smiling as he saw the whale. 'Very original.'

Max sneaked a glance at the other entries. They were all beautifully presented, but he was astonished to see how plain they were. There were squares of marzipan, and circles (in different colours), and one or two shapes that looked like flowers. But none of them – not a single one – was in the shape of an animal or fruit. His heart sank.

'We've done the wrong thing,' he said

to Herr Gross. 'All the others look much the same. Only ours is different.'

'Nonsense,' said Herr Gross, trying to sound confident, although he, too, had noticed. 'They're the ones who have done the wrong thing – not us!'

The judging of the entries took place that afternoon. The confectioners all had to stand back while the judges inspected the entries, and Max and Herr Gross found themselves next to two of their competitors. Max did not try to overhear what they were saying, but they talked so loudly that it was impossible not to pick up their comments.

'That's good stuff from Geneva,' said the man from Zürich. 'He always comes up with something interesting.'

'I agree,' replied one of the men from St Moritz. 'But as for those curious bits

and pieces from goodness knows where
. . . A whale, would you believe it! How
ridiculous! *So* old-fashioned!'

Max smarted at this remark and fixed
his gaze on the judge. Well, he thought –
we shall wait and see what the judges
think.

Slowly the three men in white coats
passed down the line of entries, making
notes in notebooks as they looked at each

exhibit. Max caught his breath as they stopped before his entry. The judges were huddled together, and spoke in low voices, but by straining his ears Max was just able to make out what they were saying.

'They're very skilfully made,' said one of them. 'Look at the way there's a little spout of water coming out of the whale's blow-hole.'

'Mmm,' said another. 'That's all very well, but people have been making marzipan animals for so long. It's really just a question of copying. There's nothing *new* about them.'

'But does that matter?' said the first judge. 'As long as people like them . . .'

'Nonsense,' chipped in the third judge, who had been silent until then. 'People must be encouraged to like new things! We can't possibly give a prize for this sort of work.'

'I agree,' said his friend. 'I'm not saying that they don't show some skill. It's just that we must get people to try new subjects for a change. If we gave prizes for marzipan animals, that is all we'd ever see. The whole country would be covered with marzipan pigs!'

'That's not true,' protested the first judge. 'Lots of people like marzipan ani-

mals, and why shouldn't they? I like these. I think they're very good.' He paused. 'But I see that you don't agree with me, so I won't press the matter.'

Max's heart sank. He could tell that the first judge really liked their work and wanted to give it a prize, but the other two had no intention of allowing that. If only there had been two who thought like the first judge, and one who thought like the others! Just as Max was thinking this, one of the judges said something which Max did not catch and the other two laughed. Then they were beyond the marzipan section . . . and looking closely at the carefully laid-out plates of chocolate.

Max knew that they had not won. But he was not prepared for what happened when the judges returned and walked briskly down the line. Every marzipan entry was given a red rosette which said on it in gold letters: *Highly commended* – except for his. The judges gave him and Herr Gross nothing – nothing at all.

# 6   A Visitor Drops In

'But they didn't even taste it!' said Max as they travelled home. 'How can they judge marzipan without tasting it?'

Herr Gross shrugged his shoulders. 'I think they had decided beforehand who would win the awards,' he commented sadly.

'That's so unfair,' Max complained.

Herr Gross agreed, but he told Max that there was nothing they could do about it. He thought the other entries were very dull, but fashions must have changed. Perhaps all the smart people in places like St Moritz and Zürich liked dull marzipan shapes these days. Perhaps nobody wanted marzipan animals any more.

Max told his parents what had happened at the competition.

'Don't be too upset,' his mother said. 'They may not like marzipan animals in St Moritz, but they certainly like them in

this valley. Everybody agrees about that.'

This was some consolation to Max, who was anyway determined not to give up. It didn't matter what people thought elsewhere; if the postman's wife liked Max's marzipan apples, then that was good enough reason to carry on making them.

So Max continued with his marzipan making, and every Saturday two trays of his wonderful little animals and pieces of fruit would be placed proudly in the window of the bakery. And by Tuesday, every one of them would have been sold, taken home, and enjoyed.

Spring came and the snows began to disappear. Now the rivers were full – rushing torrents carrying the melted snow and ice headlong down the valley. Max was busy now, as he had to help his father on the farm, do his school work, and also find time to make his weekly two trays of marzipan. It was worth it, though, and the profits from the marzipan – which Herr Gross said he should keep – were safely tucked away for when he might need any money.

One evening in the early summer, when Herr Gross had just finished a hard day's baking, he sat down on his chair by the oven and sighed.

'I don't think I can go on working much longer,' he said. 'I'm just too old. I think I'll put my feet up and retire. I've worked quite long enough.'

Max looked anxiously at the old baker. He was right, of course. All the other people of his age in the village had given up what they had used to do and now enjoyed just walking about and sitting in the sun. Herr Gross was surely entitled to do the same.

'But what about the bakery?' Max asked.

Herr Gross sighed again. 'People can get their bread from the grocery shop. They'll order it from the bakery in Santa Marta. It might not be as fresh as mine, of course, but they'll get used to it.'

Herr Gross looked up. 'I'll probably sell the bakery to one of the farmers,' he went on. 'They've been looking for a

building to store milk churns.'

Max was silent. If the bakery were to be sold, then that would mean the end of his marzipan making. There would never be room at home to make as much marzipan, as all the space in their kitchen was used up.

That week he prepared his marzipan as usual, but he did not get as much fun out of it as before. Herr Gross said nothing more about giving up the bakery, but Max could tell that he had made up his mind. And when he saw one of the farmers being shown round the shop by Herr Gross, Max knew that there was only one reason for this: the shop was definitely to be sold.

That Saturday, Herr Gross had to go to a neighbouring village to see his cousin, who was ill.

'Would you mind looking after the bakery?' he asked Max. 'You know the price of everything.'

Max was happy to help, and he spent the morning selling bread to all the usual customers. He had put a lot of effort into the marzipan pieces that week, and they sold well, too.

There was a quiet spell just before lunch and Max was just about to close up

and go home for an hour or so when the
door of the bakery opened and a woman
he had not seen before came in. The
village had one or two visitors in summer,
but not many, as it was well away from
the main road. Max thought that she
must be one of these – perhaps she was
about to hike up into the mountains and
wanted some bread for her snack.

'Those marzipan animals in the
window,' she said in a friendly voice,

pointing at Max's trays. 'Would you mind showing them to me?'

Max placed the trays in front of her and looked on proudly as she admired them.

'Why, they're wonderful!' she exclaimed. 'You don't see many marzipan figures like that these days.'

She picked up a tiny marzipan pig and popped it into her mouth.

'Don't worry,' she mumbled. 'I'll pay for it.'

As she chewed on the marzipan, she closed her eyes in ecstasy.

'And they taste *delicious*!' she went on. 'Who makes them?'

Max smiled modestly. 'I do,' he said.

The woman's eyes opened wide with surprise.

'You?' she said.

'Yes,' Max replied. 'Me.'

# 7 Word Gets Out

Max was flattered by the compliments which the visitor had paid his marzipan, and he had been pleased too when she had bought half a trayful. He thought no more of her visit, though, until some days later, when Herr Gross beckoned him eagerly into the bakery as he walked past.

'Have you seen it?' the baker said, waving a newspaper in his hand. 'I've just read it.'

'Read what?' asked Max.

Herr Gross thrust the paper into Max's

hands.

'Page four,' he said, his voice rising with excitement. 'There's an article about your marzipan – complete with photograph.'

Max turned to page four. There it was – a long article all about how the writer had wandered into a little village in a valley and found traditional marzipan pieces still being made – and by a boy! Then there was a photograph of Max's marzipan and Max immediately recognized the pieces. They were the ones bought by the woman the previous Saturday. Max had been right – she had been out on a hike – but he hadn't guessed, of course, that she was one of the editors of the newspaper.

Herr Gross cut out the article and pinned it to the front door of the bakery, where everybody could see it. It created

quite a stir and over the next few days
people stopped Max in the street to shake
his hand and congratulate him.

But something else happened, which
was far more important. The following
weekend, Max and Herr Gross began to
notice that a number of strangers came
into the bakery and asked for marzipan.
And the week after that more people
made a special journey to the village to

buy a supply. That week Max made four trays in all, and every single piece was sold.

'Do you know,' said Herr Gross. 'I think that your marzipan has become famous.'

Max laughed. 'Surely not,' he said. 'People like it, but it's not really famous.'

Herr Gross put up his hand in disagreement.

'Don't be so modest,' he said. 'It's all as a result of that newspaper article. And I shouldn't be surprised if there weren't more in the papers before too long.'

Herr Gross was right. A little while later, another writer called on Max and there followed a two page article in an important magazine. This had a tremendous effect, and Max could hardly cope with the number of people who came to the village to buy his marzipan.

This pleased the whole village. The grocery shop did well as a result, and there was even talk of opening a small café where people could have coffee and perhaps buy some of the wood carvings which a few of the old men in the village liked to make.

'You've put us on the map,' they said to Max. 'You've made the village famous!'

Max was pleased with his success, but he was still worried about what would happen when Herr Gross retired. Then, one morning, just as he was getting out of bed, an idea came to him. As he mulled it over in his mind, he wondered why he hadn't thought of it before. It was all so simple – and so obvious!

Without bothering about breakfast, Max rushed out and was soon knocking at the bakery door. He knew that Herr

Gross would be inside, baking the morning bread.

'Why, Max!' said Herr Gross as he
opened the door. 'What are you doing
here so early?'

Max drew his breath.

'Have you agreed to sell the bakery
yet?' he asked, the words all tumbling out
in a rush.

Herr Gross frowned. 'Well, I haven't
actually sold it,' he said. 'One of the

farmers is very interested in it, though.'

'I'll buy it,' said Max.

Herr Gross could not hide his astonishment. '*You'll* buy it, Max? But . . . but . . .' The old baker seemed at a loss for words.

'I can make enough money from my marzipan,' said Max. 'I'm sure I'll be able to pay for it.'

Herr Gross scratched his head. 'Well, I suppose there's no reason why not.'

'And there's another thing,' said Max, pressing on. 'When I leave school I'll re-open it as a bakery. I'll do bread *and* marzipan.'

Herr Gross's face cracked into a smile of delight. 'That's marvellous,' he said. 'I'll teach you how to bake whenever you want me to. The village will be very, very relieved!'

★  ★  ★

Herr Gross discussed the matter that evening with Max's parents. They had no objection to the sale, provided that Max only worked at weekends and left enough time for his schoolwork. Max was happy to agree to this.

After that, there was little left to be done. Max had already made enough money from marzipan to pay a good part of the price to Herr Gross, and the old baker was quite content to wait for the rest to be paid bit by bit as the marzipan sales went on. And the marzipan sales went on very well indeed as the news of Max's skill spread further and further.

At the end of that summer, Herr Gross gave up baking altogether, although not before giving Max a good number of lessons in the art of baking bread.

'Don't worry,' he reassured his pupil. 'I shall always be around in the village and you can ask my advice at any time!'

The bakery was closed down during the week, and when it opened on Saturday it was purely a marzipan shop. But it was a very busy marzipan shop and there were always people going in and out, clutching small bags and parcels of Max's wonderful marzipan.

Then, one day, Max invited Herr Gross to see a new sort of marzipan model he

was going to start making. He had covered the model with a cloth so that the old baker could unveil it himself, which he did with a flourish.

Herr Gross gasped as he saw what Max had made.

'It's Putti!' he cried out, laughing with pleasure. 'You've made my old car!'

'Yes,' said Max. 'I'm sure it'll be popular.'

And it was, particularly with Herr Gross, who called in every Saturday to buy two marzipan cars – one for his grandson, who lived at the other end of the village – and, of course, one for himself!